E.C. DOREN

Sometimes I Wonder if Poodles like Noodles

written by LAURA NUMEROFF ∞ illustrated by TIM BOWERS

Simon & Schuster Books for Young Readers

SOMETIMES I WONDER

Sometimes I wonder if poodles like noodles,
Do lions use irons,
Can chickens read Dickens,
Do horses take courses,
Can beavers be weavers,
Do monkeys ride donkeys,
Can aardvarks be card sharks,
Do rabbits break habits,
Can kittens knit mittens,
Do possums wear blossoms,
Can turtles jump hurdles?
I don't know the answers,
I haven't a clue.
It's just fun to wonder,
Do you do it, too?

Spots

My dalmatian's name is Sydney,
He's got a million spots.
I think it would be fun to try
Connecting all his dots!

A Story I Like to Tell

There's a story I tell to my family.
It always makes them laugh.
It's about a lady who's trying to knit
A scarf for a giraffe.

She knits and knits and knits all day
Until she thinks she's done.
But the giraffe's neck is much too long,
It's clear he'll need another one!

MY GRANDMA AND MY GRANDPA

Every day when the sun comes up
My grandma likes to dance.
My grandpa makes a phone call
To his best friend Jacques in France.

Then Grandpa likes to cook all day,
He says he's never bored.
My grandma plays the banjo,
But she only knows one chord.

And so she strums while Grandpa hums
And bakes his casserole.
They always eat by candlelight,
Then go out for a stroll.

And after that it's time for chess,
Their favorite game to play.
They do the same thing all week long.
They wouldn't have it any other way.

My Cousin's New Paint Set

My cousin got a paint set,
Some paper and an easel.
She painted a giant picture
Of a polka-dotted weasel.

When she was done she signed her name
And began to paint again.
This time it was a classroom
And the teacher was a hen.

She painted red dogs and hot pink cats
And a pair of orange pigs,
Lime green bears and light blue cows
And turquoise monkeys wearing wigs.

She also painted purple frogs
And a red-and-white-striped horse
But the one I like the most of all
Is the one of me, of course!

MY FRIEND'S FRECKLES

My best friend, Kate, has red hair and freckles
That cover her cheeks and her nose.
The first time I met her I had to ask,
"Do your freckles go down to your toes?"

SLEEPOVER

Once in a while
My friend spends the night.
We get under a blanket
And use a flashlight.

We read from my book
About a house with a ghost
Until it scares us too much,
Then we go have some toast.

When we finish our snack
We get back in our beds.
And then we tell stories
From out of our heads.

This time the monsters
Don't give us a fright.
We hold tight to our pillows
And leave on the light!

On Halloween

On Halloween I like to see
What everyone pretends to be.
Ghosts and monsters and scary ghouls,
Pirates and maidens with beautiful jewels.

Cowgirls and princes and black pussycats,
Horses and pumpkins, witches and bats.
Gypsies and lizards, martians and pigs,
Werewolves and tigers, ballerinas in wigs.

This year I'm going as corn on the cob.
Making my costume was quite a hard job.
I pasted hundreds of squares onto my clothes.
I'm covered with them from my head to my toes.

DINOSAUR BONES

I like to go to the science museum
And see the dinosaur's bones.
He looks like he could have eaten
A million ice-cream cones.

I stand below and look straight up,
He's at least eight stories tall.
I have all of my toes and my fingers crossed
That nothing will make him fall.

LEARNING TO ICE-SKATE

I'm learning how to ice-skate,
But I'm always falling down.
I guess it's lucky that I'm short,
So I'm closer to the ground.

I'd like to spin around and round,
And do a figure eight.
But I'll have to start with staying up—
Figure eights can wait.

WHEN I WAS SICK IN BED

Last week at school I caught a cold
And had to stay in bed.
I drank hot tea, took vitamin C,
And read and read and read.

I read biographies and fairy tales,
And a book about the sea.
I read poetry and picture books
And a spooky mystery.

I was so busy reading, actually,
Being sick didn't bother me!

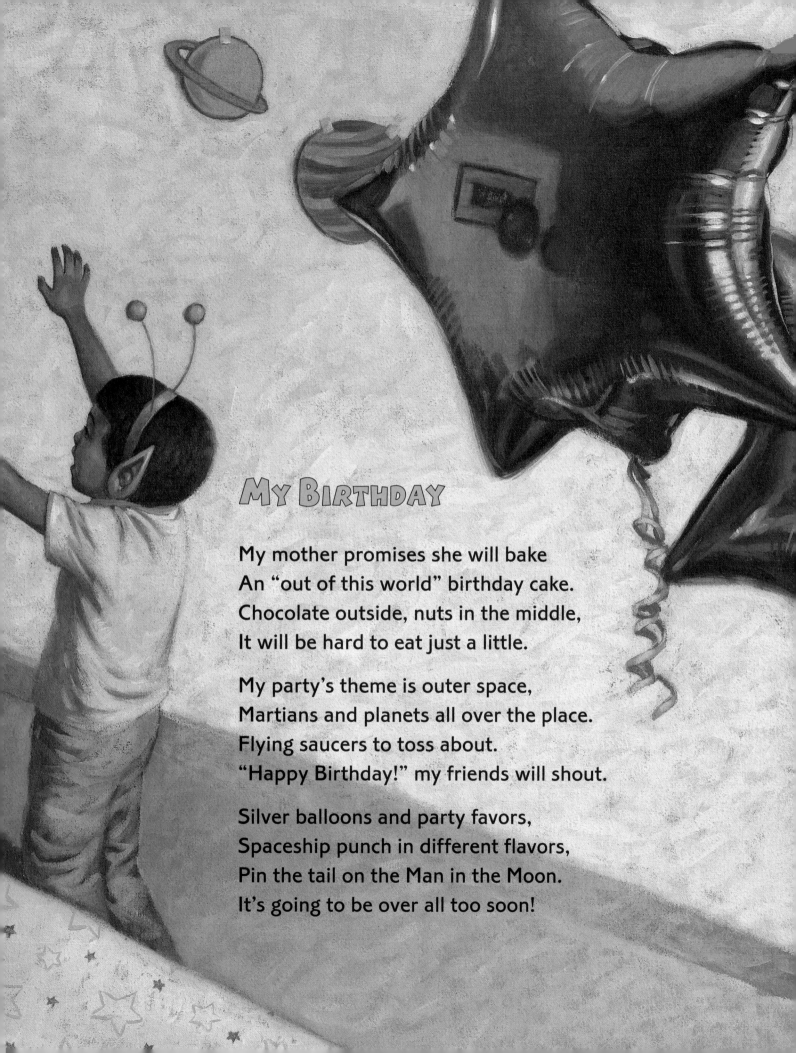

My Birthday

My mother promises she will bake
An "out of this world" birthday cake.
Chocolate outside, nuts in the middle,
It will be hard to eat just a little.

My party's theme is outer space,
Martians and planets all over the place.
Flying saucers to toss about.
"Happy Birthday!" my friends will shout.

Silver balloons and party favors,
Spaceship punch in different flavors,
Pin the tail on the Man in the Moon.
It's going to be over all too soon!

A Day at the Beach

This summer when I go to the beach
I'd like to collect some shells.
I'll string them together and hang them at home
So when the wind blows they'll sound like bells.

I'd also like to play tag with the waves
(To see if they can catch me).
I know I'm too fast but I'll give them a chance.
Have you ever been tagged by the sea?

Then I want to build in the sand,
This time I might try a big car.
When it's all done I'll sit in the front,
But I don't expect to get very far.

I can fly my homemade kite,
Draw birds or planes with my hand.
I can fill up my pail with things that I find
Or bury my feet in the sand.

I'll lie in the sun and take a short nap
And when I wake up we'll be on our way.
Then every time my shell chimes tinkle
I'll remember my most perfect day.

I Like to Cook

Sometimes I make lunch by myself,
To help my mother out.
I make beef stew in the microwave,
With yams and sauerkraut.
I make ham and tuna sandwiches,
With butter and tomato,
Or chunky peanut butter
Or half a baked potato.
I always have some carrot juice
Or chocolate milk to drink.
I'm getting to be a very good cook,
At least that's what I think!

BAKING FUN

Every so often my dad and I bake.
We make chocolate chip cookies
Or three-layer cake.

We sing silly songs while we measure and pour
And Sydney, our dog, sleeps nearby on the floor.

When everything's finished
And ready to eat,
The two of us sit down
(Sydney sits by our feet).

We enjoy the warm cookies
Or huge slices of cake,
Never rushing to clean up
The big messes we make.

DUETS

My mother and I play piano,
We have a favorite song.
She plays left and I play right
And our dog will sing along.

Often we get all mixed up
And play each other's part.
We laugh so hard we have to stop
And go back to the start.

We love to play together,
Duets are so much fun.
Sometimes we give a concert
And Dad claps when we're done.

Bath Time

In the evening I take my bath
And pretend I'm in a boat,
Or bring in different toys
To see if they can float.

I have a plastic dolphin
That putters all around.
And a floating helicopter
That doesn't make a sound.

I like to build shampoo horns
And pretend that I'm a bull.
Or fill the tub with bubbles
Until it's almost full.

I use every inch of towel,
to make sure that I'm dry.
My fingers look like raisins,
But I have no clue why.

I crawl into my pj's
And brush-brush-brush my teeth,
Then I pull back all my covers
And crawl in underneath.

My New Pajamas

These days I wear pj's
That I think are rather neat.
They're new and blue with polka dots
And come complete with feet.

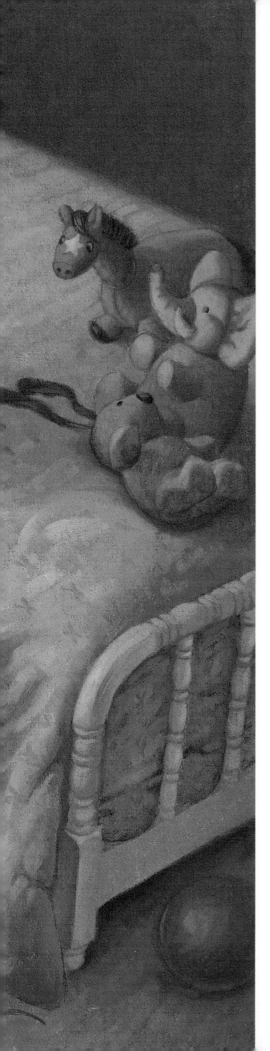

GOOD NIGHT

Every night before I sleep
I have to say "good night"
To all my toys and animals,
Or else I don't feel right.

I have so many in my room,
It seems to take all night,
Till mom says it's getting late
And then shuts off the light.

I always say, "I forgot someone."
She always answers, "Who?"
I put my arms around her neck
And whisper, "I love you!"

MY WONDERFUL DREAM

Last night I had the strangest dream,
That I was on a whale.
We took a trip around the world,
With me upon his tail.

We went to Bali and Peru,
To Italy and France.
We saw a school of foreign fish,
And watched a mermaid dance.

We drank green tea in China,
In England we munched scones.
We made a stop in Amsterdam,
For Dutch chocolate ice-cream cones.

We went all the way to Africa
To see zebras and giraffes,
And the muddy hippopotamus
Gave us a lot of laughs.

Then on we went to India
To try a taste of curry.
We took our time getting home,
We weren't in a hurry.

And when our trip came to an end,
I thanked him for the ride.
I told him how much fun I'd had,
And that he was the perfect guide!

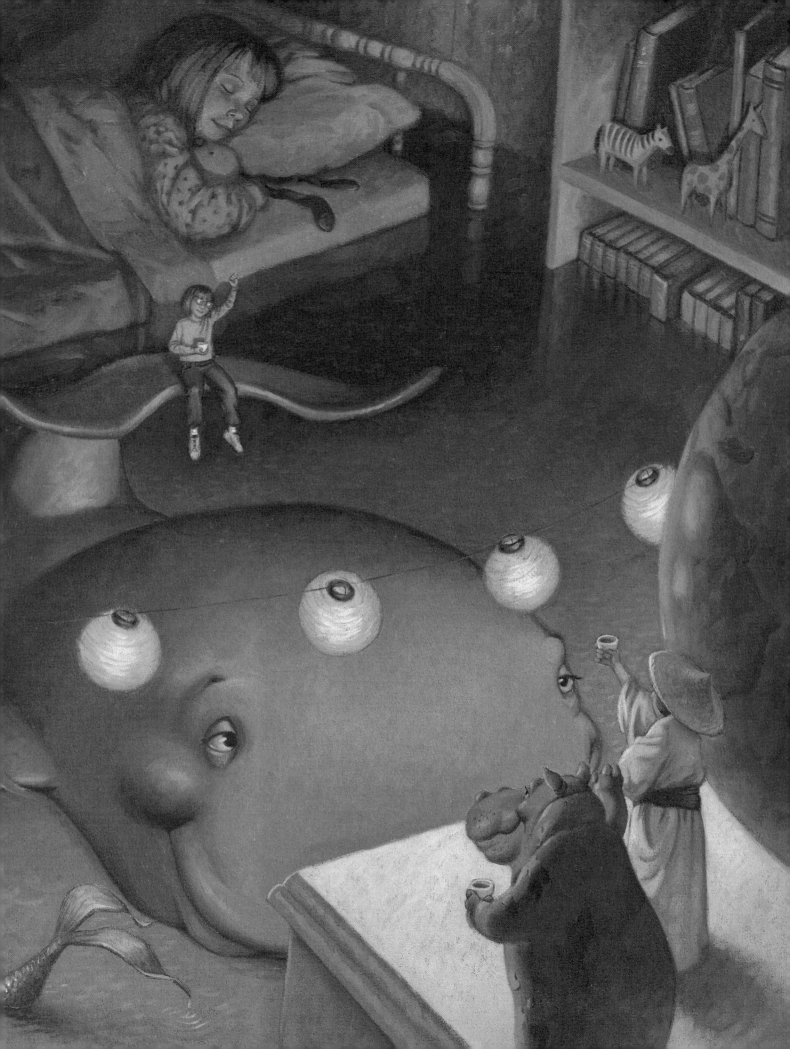

P.S. Did You Know?

Did you know that camels sway and horses neigh,
Puppies yap and kittens nap,
Bullfrogs leap and hamsters sleep,
Monkeys swing and possums cling,
Tadpoles grow and roosters crow,
Crickets chirp and piglets slurp,
Eagles soar and lions roar,
Bedbugs bite and fireflies light?

Now you do.

For Lisa, Lois, and my horse, Otis, at Freeway Farms—
thank you for everything, especially your patience
—L.N.

To Allison, Jon, Megan, and Brynne for being such great models,
and to my childhood oil-painting teacher, Mrs. Edith Marvel,
with appreciation and fond memories
—T.B.

SIMON & SCHUSTER BOOKS FOR YOUNG READERS
An imprint of Simon & Schuster Children's Publishing Division
1230 Avenue of the Americas, New York, NY 10020
Text copyright © 1999 by Laura Numeroff
Illustrations copyright © 1999 by Tim Bowers
All rights reserved including the right of reproduction in whole or in part in any form.
SIMON & SCHUSTER BOOKS FOR YOUNG READERS is a trademark of Simon & Schuster.

Book design by Anahid Hamparian
The text of this book is set in 17-point Corinthian.

Printed in Hong Kong
First Edition
10 9 8 7 6 5 4 3 2 1

Library of Congress Cataloging-in-Publication Data
Numeroff, Laura Joffe.
Sometimes I wonder if poodles like noodles / by Laura Numeroff ; illustrated by Tim Bowers.
p.   cm.
Summary: An illustrated collection of humorous verses about a child's day-to-day experiences and other topics.
ISBN 0-689-80563-2
1. Humorous poetry, American. 2. Children's poetry, American. [1. American poetry. 2. Humorous poetry.]
I. Bowers, Tim, ill.   II. Title.   PS3564.U45S66 1999   811'.54—dc21   96-44988   CIP   AC

The illustrations are rendered in oil paint on canvas.